SEA TURTLES

ASHLEY GISH

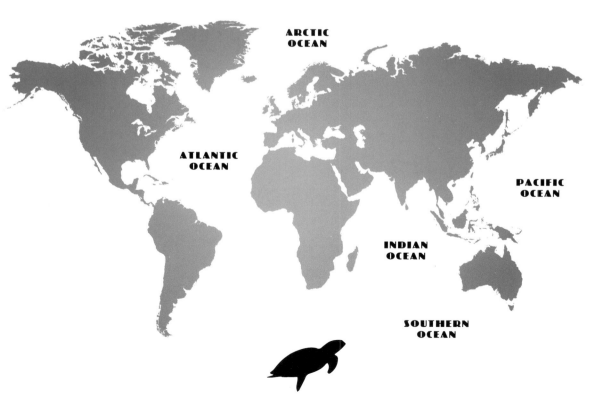

ARCTIC
OCEAN

ATLANTIC
OCEAN

PACIFIC
OCEAN

INDIAN
OCEAN

SOUTHERN
OCEAN

CREATIVE EDUCATION · CREATIVE PAPERBACKS

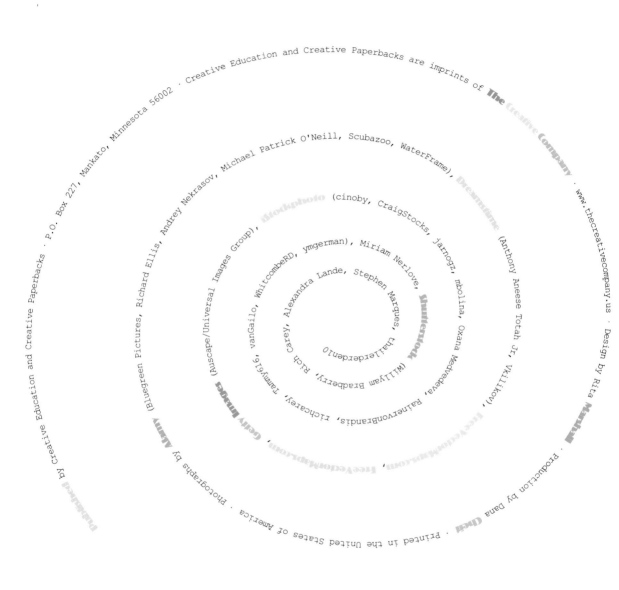

Published by Creative Education and Creative Paperbacks · P.O. Box 227, Mankato, Minnesota 56002 · Creative Education and Creative Paperbacks are imprints of The Creative Company · www.thecreativecompany.us · Design by Rita Marshall · Production by Dana Cheit · Printed in the United States of America · Photographs by Alamy (Bluegreen Pictures, Richard Ellis, Andrey Nekrasov, Michael Patrick O'Neill, Scubazoo, WaterFrame), Dreamstime (Anthony Aneese Totah Jr, Vkilikov), freevectormaps.com, Getty Images (Auscape/Universal Images Group), iStockphoto (cinoby, CraigStocks, jarnogz, mbolina, Oxana Medvedeva, RainervonBrandis, richcarey, TammyE19, vanGailo, WhitcombeRD, ymgerman), Miriam Nerlove, Shutterstock (William Bradberry, Rich Carey, Alexandra Lande, Stephen Marques, thalerdeden10)

Library of Congress Cataloging-in-Publication Data • Names: Gish, Ashley, author. • Title: Sea Turtles / Ashley Gish. • Series: X-Books: Reptiles. • Summary: A countdown of five of the most fascinating sea turtles provides thrills as readers learn about the biological, social, and hunting characteristics of these flippered, ocean-dwelling reptiles. • Identifiers: ISBN 978-1-64026-084-9 (hardcover) / ISBN 978-1-62832-672-7 (pbk) / ISBN 978-1-64000-200-5 (eBook) • This title has been submitted for CIP processing under LCCN 2018939091. • CCSS: RI.3.1-8; RI.4.1-5, 7; RI.5.1-3, 8; RI.6.1-2, 4, 7; RH.6-8.3-8
First Edition HC 9 8 7 6 5 4 3 2 1 • First Edition PBK 9 8 7 6 5 4 3 2 1

SEA TURTLES

CONTENTS

Xciting **FACTS 28**

Xceptional **REPTILES 5**

Xtreme **TOP 5 SEA TURTLES**

#5 **10**
#4 **16**
#3 **22**
#2 **26**
#1 **31**

Xasperating **CONFLICT 24**

Xemplary **SKILLS 20**

Xtraordinary **LIFESTYLE**

GLOSSARY

RESOURCES

INDEX 32

REPTILES BOOKS

gunnison county **Libraries**
connect. discover. imagine. learn.

Gunnison Library
307 N. Wisconsin, Gunnison, CO 81230
970.641.3485
www.gunnisoncountylibraries.org

SEA TURTLE SPECIES

LEATHERBACK

KEMP'S RIDLEY

HAWKSBILL

FLATBACK

GREEN

LOGGERHEAD

OLIVE RIDLEY

XCEPTIONAL REPTILES

Sea turtles live in the sea. They use their flippers to swim. They can stay underwater for hours. Some travel all around the world's oceans.

Sea Turtle Basics

There are seven kinds of sea turtles. They all live in the ocean. But they must breathe air. They rise to the surface to breathe. Sea turtles hold their breath while swimming underwater. They have spongy tissue in their mouths and throats. This tissue soaks up oxygen from the water.

Sea turtles are **reptiles**. Their body temperature changes with their surroundings. They swim near the water's surface to warm up in the sunshine. To cool off, they dive deep underwater.

WORLDWIDE SEA TURTLES

sea turtle range

SMALLEST KINDS

At less than 100 pounds (45.4 kg)
and 23 to 28 inches (58.4–71.1 cm)
long, Kemp's and olive ridley
sea turtles are the smallest.

LARGEST KIND

Leatherbacks are the largest
sea turtles, at about 2,000 pounds
(907 kg) and more than six feet (1.8 m) long.

SENSITIVE SHELLS

Sea turtles can feel any touch on their shells.

TRAVELING FLATBACKS

Flatback sea turtles migrate only around Australia.

AUSTRALIA

Flatback, green, hawksbill, loggerhead, Kemp's ridley, and olive ridley sea turtles have hard shells. Leatherbacks do not have bony shells. They have thick, leathery skin instead.

SEA TURTLE SHELLS

Sea turtles have four flippers. The flippers work like canoe paddles. They push the sea turtle through the water.

Sea turtles filter the seawater they drink. They get rid of the salt they swallow through tiny openings around their eyes. Clear eye coverings help them see underwater.

Sea turtles have a special **organ** in their mouth. It captures scents in the water. They can smell food from far away.

Sea turtles can go weeks without food.

SKIPPING X MEALS

SEA TURTLE BASICS FACT

The upper part of the shell is called
the carapace. The underside is the plastron.

TOP FIVE XTREME SEA TURTLES

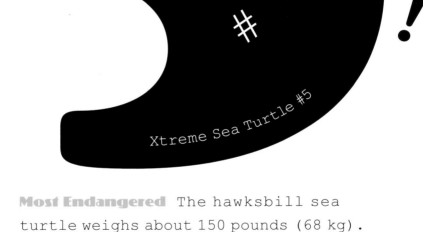

Xtreme Sea Turtle #5

Most Endangered The hawksbill sea turtle weighs about 150 pounds (68 kg). Its golden-brown shell is 30 to 39 inches (76.2–99.1 cm) long. It has a striking pattern of brown, orange, red, and black. People use these beautiful shells to make hair clips, jewelry, and other ornaments. These items are called "tortoiseshell." This is why the hawksbill sea turtle is the most at risk of dying out.

Sea turtles normally hold their breath four to five minutes

when swimming underwater.

Sea Turtle Babies

Sea turtle babies hatch from eggs. At night, mother sea turtles drag themselves onto sandy shores. They dig holes with their front flippers. Then they lay as many as 200 eggs. They bury the group of eggs, called a clutch. Females lay up to eight clutches one to two weeks apart. Then they return to sea. They will not mate again for two or three years.

The eggs stay warm and safe in the sand. In the center of the clutch, the eggs are warmer. These will develop into females. On the outer edges, the eggs are cooler. These will become males. The babies grow inside the eggs for 45 to 80 days. They are about two inches (5.1 cm) long when they hatch.

After hatching, they work together. They begin to dig their way out of the nest. When the hatchlings feel the cool temperature above them, they know it is nighttime. They burst from the nest. They head toward the brightest light they see: the moon. They race across the sand toward the sea.

up to
200
eggs

45
to
80
days

| Mother lays eggs | Babies grow inside eggs | Eggs hatch |

14.2 to

0.5 to **1.5** ounces

42.5 g

20 years

Hatchlings head for sea

Turtles reproduce

30 years

SEA TURTLE BABIES FACT

Many hatchlings die racing toward lights

on beachfront buildings instead of the moon.

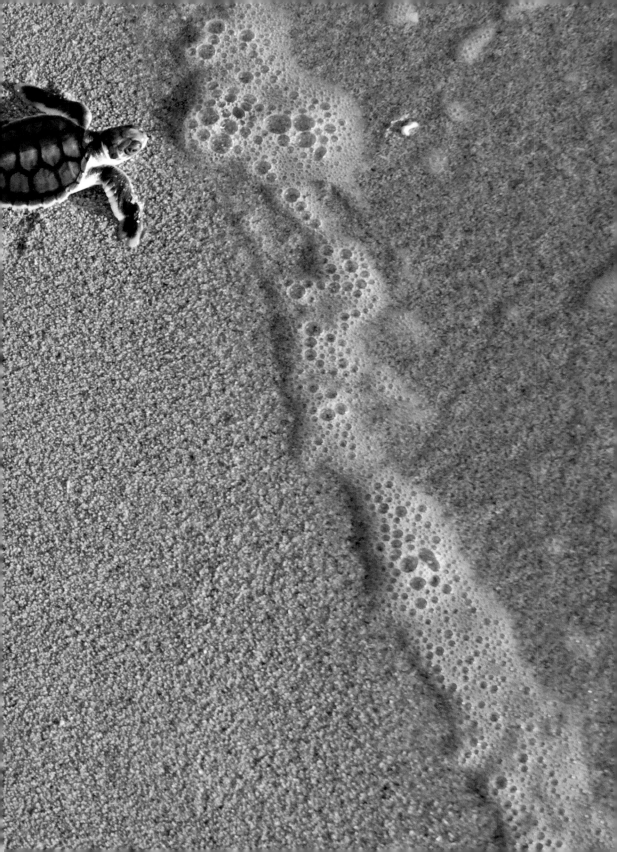

TOP FIVE XTREME SEA TURTLES

Xtreme Sea Turtle #4

Largest Leatherback The largest sea turtle ever recorded was a leatherback. It drowned in 1988 after being trapped in a fishing line. It washed ashore in Wales. The National Museum in Cardiff studied it. Researchers determined that it was 100 years old! It was nearly 9.8 feet (3 m) long. It weighed 2,016 pounds (914 kg). Specialists preserved the sea turtle. It is now on display at the museum.

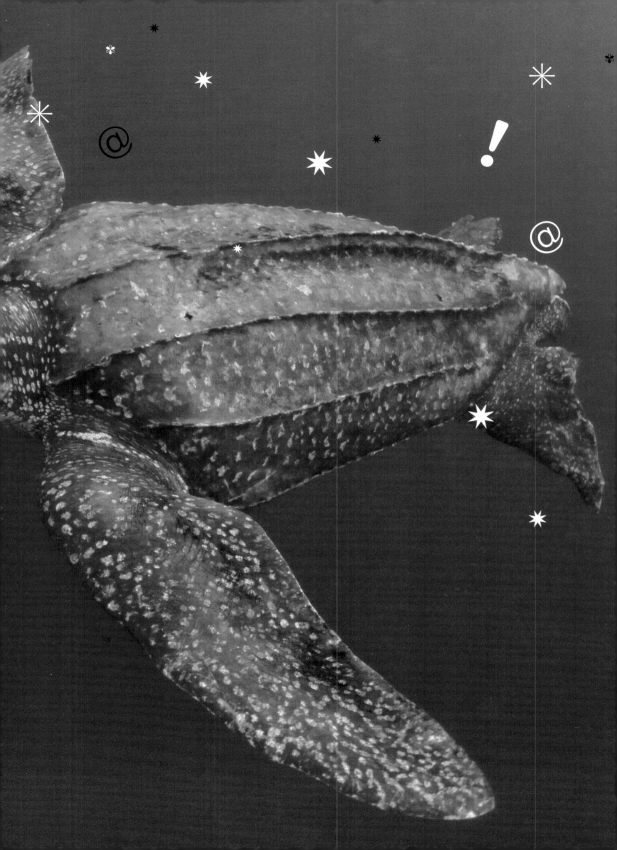

XTRAORDINARY LIFESTYLE

Sea turtles are perfectly at home in the vast ocean. They are adapted to life on their own. They have many defenses. They swim quickly. Their shells help keep them safe.

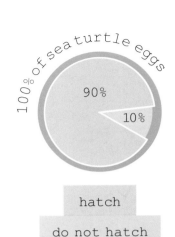

100% of sea turtle eggs

90%

10%

hatch

do not hatch

SEA TURTLE SOCIETY FACT

Sea turtles visit coral reef cleaning stations.

Cleaner fish eat parasites off their shells, heads, and limbs.

Some sea turtles can live 100 years.

LONG X LIVES

Sea Turtle Society

Sea turtles migrate. They travel the world's oceans. They live alone. Every few years, they come together to mate. Hundreds of females may gather to lay eggs in the same place at the same time.

Sea turtles follow ocean currents. They ride in these fast-flowing waters. This keeps them from getting too tired. Most sea turtles cruise along at about two miles (3.2 km) per hour. Leatherbacks can swim almost six miles (9.7 km) per hour.

Sea turtles visit coral reefs. Hawksbill sea turtles eat sea sponges. This keeps sponges from overcrowding the reef. It helps the reef stay healthy. Too much algae and too many jellyfish can also be damaging. Green sea turtles eat sea grasses and algae. Leatherback sea turtles eat jellyfish.

XEMPLARY SKILLS

Tiny hatchlings are not strong swimmers. They drift on ocean currents. But adults are powerful swimmers. They navigate around the world's oceans.

XEMPLARY SKILLS FACT

To stay at the water's surface, young sea turtles fill their lungs with air like floaties.

Flatback sea turtles have thinner shells than other sea turtles. This puts them at greater risk of being attacked.

EARTH'S
MAGNETIC ——
FIELD

Sea turtles can sense Earth's magnetic field. (This is the area around a magnetic object that guides the pull or push of the object in a particular direction.) Scientists believe sea turtles use the magnetic field to navigate Earth's oceans.

Sea turtles use this amazing sense to remember the best feeding grounds. They also make their way to cleaning stations on coral reefs. When the time comes to lay eggs, females find the beaches where they hatched. There, they lay their own eggs.

Xtreme Sea Turtle #3

Traveing Turtle A female loggerhead holds the record for the longest known sea turtle migration. Scientists glued a device to her shell. This allowed them to follow her movements. They tracked her voyage from nesting grounds in Indonesia to Oregon. Then she went to Hawaii and back to Indonesia. She traveled 12,774 miles (20,558 km) in 674 days. Scientists are not sure why sea turtles travel so much. Maybe they have favorite feeding spots around the world!

XASPERATING CONFLICT

Sea turtles face many challenges. Climate change and pollution are affecting the oceans. Sea turtles are getting sick. Humans are invading their nesting and hatching grounds. Sea turtles can be killed in encounters with humans.

Sea Turtle Survival

Young sea turtles hide from predators in floating mats of algae. Adult sea turtles are hunted by great white and tiger sharks. They hide under ledges of rock or coral. When resting, sea turtles can stay underwater for up to six hours. Spongy tissue in the mouth and throat absorbs oxygen from the water.

Sea turtles have sharp beaks. Beaks can be used for defense. Mostly, they are used to slice or crush food. Flatback sea turtles eat sea cucumbers and other spineless creatures. Kemp's and olive ridleys eat crabs and clams. So do loggerheads.

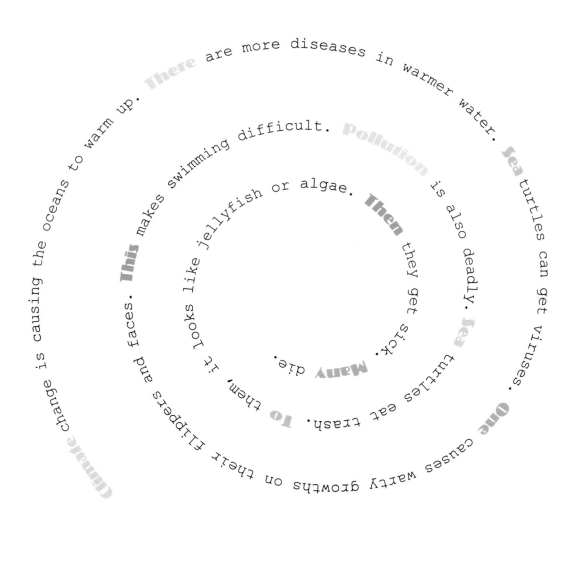

Climate change is causing the oceans to warm up. There are more diseases in warmer water. Sea turtles can get viruses. One causes warty growths on their flippers and faces. This makes swimming difficult. Pollution is also deadly. Sea turtles eat trash. To them, it looks like jellyfish or algae. Then they get sick. Many die.

SEA TURTLE SURVIVAL FACT

Many sea turtles drown after getting caught in large fishing nets.

Xtreme Sea Turtle #2

Baffling Behavior Sea turtles do not normally **hibernate**. But in 1976, a group of sea turtles was found near Baja California, Mexico. They had buried themselves in mud. They came to the surface to breathe only once per day. In 1980, a second group was found. This group was off the coast of Cape Canaveral, Florida. They were hibernating, too. Sea turtles still hibernate in these two places. Scientists have no idea why!

XCITING FACTS

Fewer than 23,000 nesting female hawksbill sea turtles remain on the planet today.

If sea turtles get too cold, they cannot digest their food. They can die as a result.

The gathering of nesting females is called an arribada. It is Spanish for "arrival."

Sea turtle eggs look like Ping-Pong balls. They are soft and rubbery.

Kemp's ridleys are the only female sea turtles that nest every year.

Powerful hurricanes can drown sea turtles and destroy their nests

Sea turtles may rub against rocks or hard corals to loosen pesky parasites.

The leatherback sea turtle is the fourth-heaviest reptile in the world

Sea turtles may grow 70 times bigger during their first 10 years of life.

As adults, green sea turtles eat only plants and algae.

On their race to the ocean, about one-third of hatchlings are eaten by predators.

Some sea turtles reach adulthood at age 50 and can live more than 100 years.

Australia's saltwater crocodiles sometimes hunt sea turtles.

Green and loggerhead sea turtles weigh up to 400 pounds (181 kg).

Their shells can be four feet (1.2 m) long.

TOP FIVE XTREME SEA TURTLES

Xtreme Sea Turtle #1

Largest Arribada Costa Rica's Ostional Wildlife Refuge was created in 1984. Olive ridley sea turtles nest on the beaches there. A few weeks before nesting, thousands of sea turtles gather offshore. This group is called a flotilla. They float together. Then the female sea turtles come ashore to nest. The largest arribada ever recorded happened at Ostional in 1995. About 500,000 olive ridley sea turtles gathered. They laid about 10 million eggs!

GLOSSARY

hibernate – spend the winter in a sleep-like state in which breathing and heart rate slow down

migrate – move from one place to another, usually regularly by the seasons

navigate – plan and follow a course of travel

organ – a part of a living being that performs a specific task in the body

parasites – animals or plants that live on or inside another living thing (called a host) while giving nothing back to the host; some parasites cause disease or even death

reptiles – animals with dry, scaly skin whose body temperatures change with their surroundings.

RESOURCES

"Green Sea Turtle." National Geographic Kids. https://kids.nationalgeographic.com/animals/green-sea-turtle/#green-sea-turtle-closeup-underwater.jpg.

"Sea Turtles Facts." Active Wild: Wildlife & Science Facts. http://www.activewild.com/sea-turtles-facts/.

Swinburne, Stephen R. *Sea Turtle Scientist*. New York: Houghton Mifflin Harcourt, 2014.

Young, Karen Romano. *Mission: Sea Turtle Rescue*. Washington, D.C.: National Geographic Kids, 2015.

INDEX

arribadas 19, 28, 31

coral reefs 18, 19, 21

diets 19, 24, 25, 28

eggs 12, 18, 19, 21, 28, 31

hatchlings 12, 14, 20, 25, 28

physical features 5, 7, 8, 9, 10, 12, 18, 20, 24, 25

senses 7, 8, 9, 12, 21

species 5, 6, 7, 8, 10, 16, 19, 20, 22, 24, 28, 31

swimming 5, 8, 11, 18, 19, 20, 22, 25

threats 10, 14, 16, 20, 24, 25, 28

Sea turtle relatives began to grow shells about 260 million years ag